RAIN!

To my rain-loving friend Kathleen Pelley, with thanks and admiration.
—L.A.

To Nigel, Nana, and Mama for being the sun
that is always shining above the rain clouds.
—C.R.

Text copyright © 2013 by Linda Ashman
Illustrations copyright © 2013 by Christian Robinson

Houghton Mifflin Books for Children is an imprint of Houghton Mifflin Harcourt
Publishing Company.

www.hmhbooks.com

The text of this book is set in Rockwell, Bryant, and Adobe Caslon Pro.
The illustrations are paint and collage with digital editing.

Library of Congress Cataloging-in-Publication Data
Ashman, Linda.
Rain! / written by Linda Ashman ; illustrated by Christian Robinson.
p. cm.
Summary: As an old man grumbles his way through a rainy morning,
spreading gloom, his neighbor, a young child, spreads cheer while hopping
through puddles in frog-themed rainwear.
ISBN 978-0-547-73395-1
[1. Mood (Psychology)—Fiction. 2. Rain—Fiction. 3. Neighbors—Fiction.]
I. Robinson, Christian, ill. II. Title.
PZ7.A82675Rai 2013
[E]—dc23
2011042039

Manufactured in China
SCP 10 9 8 7 6 5 4 3 2
4500403781

RAIN!

STORY BY
LINDA ASHMAN

PICTURES BY
CHRISTIAN ROBINSON

HOUGHTON MIFFLIN BOOKS FOR CHILDREN
Houghton Mifflin Harcourt
Boston   New York

"Nasty galoshes."

"Blasted overcoat."

"There goes
my hair . . ."

"Is it raining cats and dogs?"

"It's raining frogs and pollywogs!"

"Hippity-hop!"

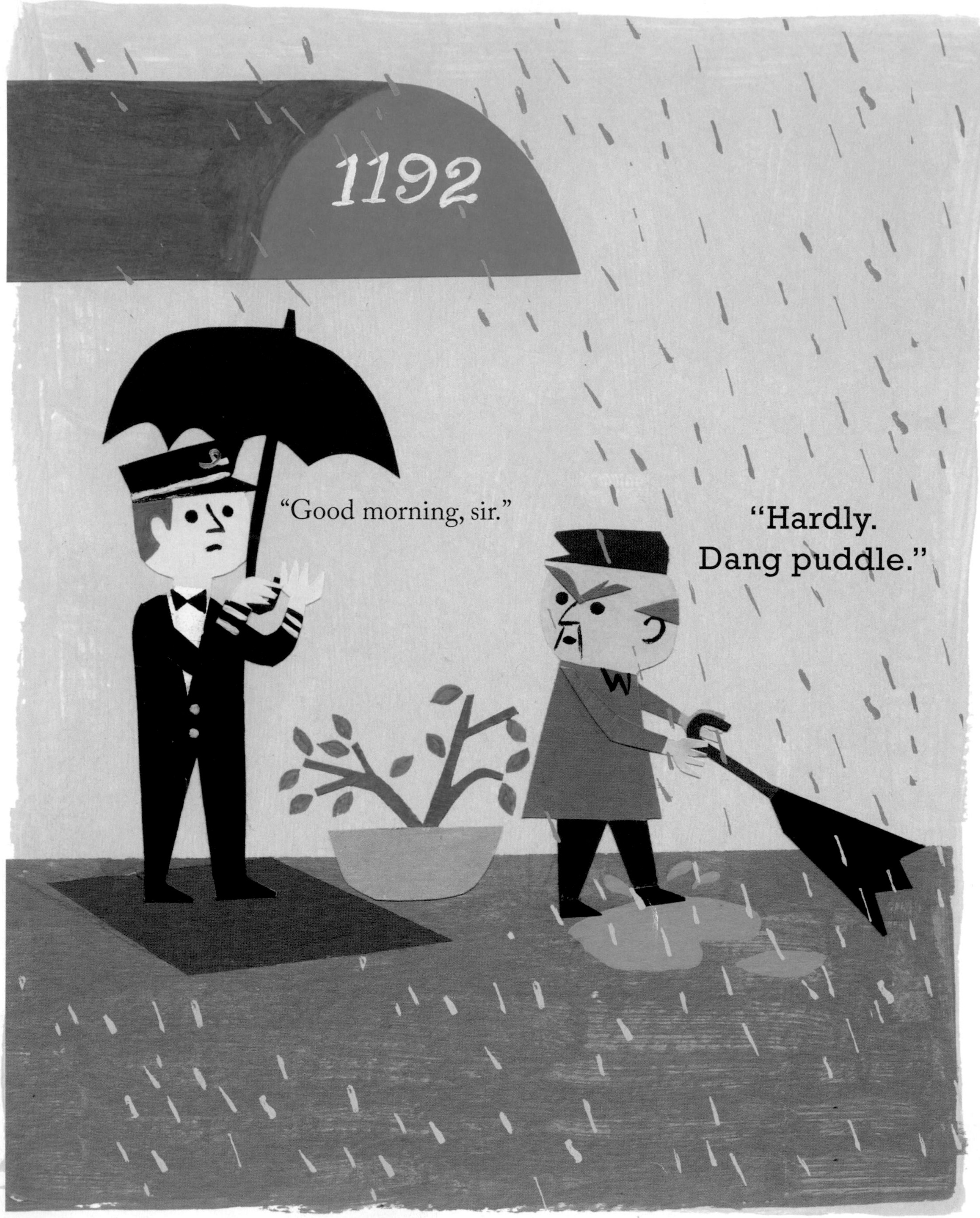

"Good morning, sir."

"Hardly.
Dang puddle."

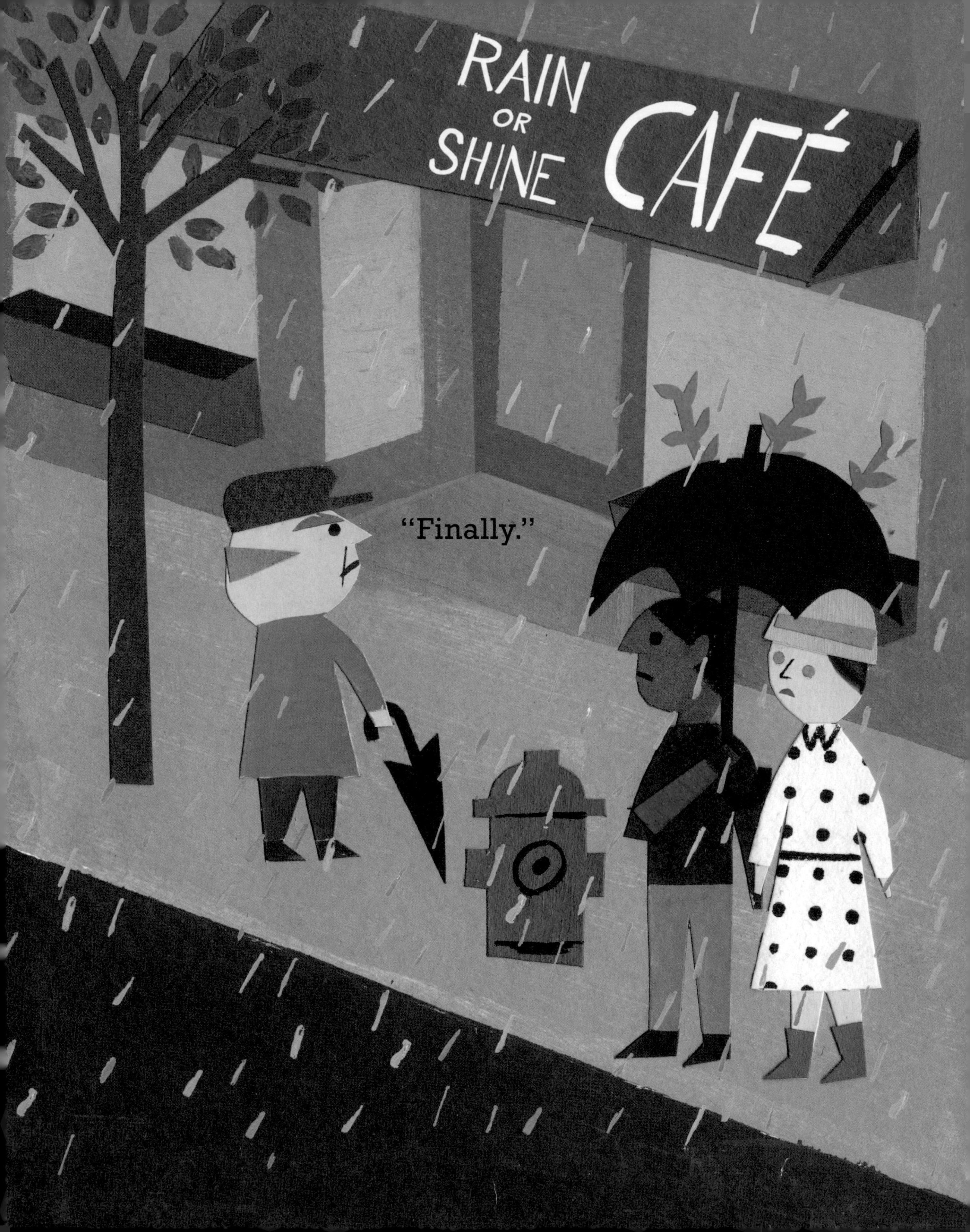
RAIN OR SHINE CAFÉ
"Finally."

"Cocoa and cookies, please."

"His hat!"

"Hey, wait!"

"You?"

"You!"

"That one, too."

"Mine?"

"Ribbit?"